Lazy Jack

and other stories

Miles Kelly

First published in 2011 by Miles Kelly Publishing Ltd
Harding's Barn, Bardfield End Green, Thaxted, Essex, CM6 3PX, UK

2 4 6 8 10 9 7 5 3 1

Publishing Director Belinda Gallagher

Creative Director Jo Cowan

Editor Amanda Askew

Senior Designer Joe Jones

Designer Kayleigh Allen

Production Manager Elizabeth Collins

Reprographics Anthony Cambray, Stephan Davis, Jennifer Hunt

ISBN 978-1-84810-441-9

Printed in China

British Library Cataloguing-in-Publication Data
A catalogue record for this book is available from the British Library

ACKNOWLEDGEMENTS
Artworks are from the Miles Kelly Artwork Bank

Made with paper from a sustainable forest

www.mileskelly.net
info@mileskelly.net

www.factsforprojects.com

Self-publish your
children's book

buddingpress.co.uk

Contents

The Pied Piper of Hamelin

An Irish folk tale

Imagine what it would be like to live in a town overrun by rats. Rats in the streets, shops and gardens! Rats in the town hall, hospital and police station! Rats in your school corridors, classroom and desk! Rats in your kitchen, bath and bed! Well, that's what it was like to live in the town of Hamelin, which lay beside the River Weser.

No one knew where the rats had come from or how they had managed to take over the town in

4

such numbers. The townspeople of Hamelin were desperate to be rid of them. They couldn't eat without rats nibbling off their plates. They couldn't get dressed without uncovering rats nesting in their clothes and boots. They couldn't put their babies down to sleep without finding rats cuddled up in the cradles. They couldn't even chat to each other in comfort, for the noise of all the squeaking and scampering.

So you can see why the mayor put up a poster outside the town hall saying:

There will be a reward of ONE THOUSAND GUILDERS to anyone who can get rid of the rats!

Yes, one thousand guilders! Everyone began to imagine what they would do with such a huge fortune – but of course, they could only dream. No one had the first idea how to begin claiming back their town from the rats.

By the time the stranger came knocking on the door of the town hall, the mayor was panic-stricken. He would have listened to anybody who said they could help. So when the stranger announced confidently, "I can get rid of all the rats for you," the mayor didn't worry too much about the stranger's odd, multicoloured costume. The mayor paid no attention to the stranger's extraordinarily long fingers and the unusual pipe that hung on a cord round his neck. The mayor didn't think too much about the sad smile on the stranger's face or the wistful gleam in his eyes. The mayor just beamed with relief.

"Right now," replied the stranger, and he raised his pipe to his lips. Off he went, out of the town hall and into the street, playing a lilting tune that filled

 6

the air. Instantly, the rats stopped scuffling, pricked up their ears, and listened. For the first time in many, many months, there was silence for a moment. Then the scampering and squeaking began again, as the rats followed the Pied Piper.

The townspeople of Weser couldn't believe their eyes. All through the town strolled the Pied Piper, his fingers continually moving on his pipe and the haunting notes rippling through the air. And out of all the houses swarmed the rats; out of every garden and gutter, out of every nook and cranny they came streaming. Down stairwells and through streets, out of passages and alleyways, over rooftops and along roads the rats came hurrying after the strange musician. And the Pied Piper didn't stop playing all the way

 7

to the wide River Weser. He didn't stop playing as he dipped one brightly coloured foot into the rushing waters and the thousands of rats began to plunge off the bank into the river. He didn't stop playing until the very last rat had drowned.

Then the church bells rang out in celebration, the townspeople hugged each other, the children danced and sang – and the Pied Piper strode quietly back to the town hall to fetch his reward.

"My one thousand guilders, if you please," said the Pied Piper, calmly.

The mayor just smiled what he thought was a charming smile. Now the rats were dead and gone he certainly didn't plan on giving away what was nearly the entire contents of the town council bank account! "Come, come now, my dear fellow," the mayor coaxed. "One thousand guilders is somewhat over-the-top for playing a pretty ditty

 8

on a tin whistle, surely you'll agree! Why don't we settle on fifty guilders, and I'll throw in a nice bronze medal and even put up a statue of you and me together in the market place, eh?"

The Pied Piper simply turned on his heel and walked out into the street. As he went, he once more lifted his pipe to his lips. But this time, he played a different tune. Enchanting notes rippled all around and down the roads the children came dancing, running and leaping after the Pied Piper.

The men and women of Hamelin were struck still with horror as the children swept past them and were gone through the town. Playing his strange melody, the Pied Piper led the children past the River Weser and skipping happily along a path that led up to a steep, craggy mountain. He piped a burst of airy notes and a little door appeared in the mountain slope. The Pied Piper led the children inside. The townspeople could hear the echo of his pipe and the children's laughter grow fainter and fainter as they went deeper and deeper into the earth. Then suddenly, the little door slammed shut and disappeared. The children were gone – all except for one little boy who was lame and so hadn't been able to keep up with the others. He stood on the mountainside and sobbed, calling out for his friends. But the little door had vanished.

No one ever saw the Pied Piper or the children again. But on sunny days, some townsfolk swore they could hear ripples of childish laughter floating down from the mountain. And from that day to this, there has never been a single rat in the town of Hamelin.

The Greedy Dog

An English tale

There was once a very greedy dog who just ate and ate. Whenever he saw anything that looked good enough to eat, he would just open his mouth and gobble it all up. The postman wouldn't come near the house anymore, ever since the greedy dog mistook his ankle for an early breakfast. He would stand at the gate and throw the letters in the general direction of the letterbox. The paperboy just refused to go anywhere near.

Visitors knew they had to come with a juicy bone or they wouldn't get as far as the front door.

One day, the greedy dog was out wandering round the shops. He loved doing this as there were always lots of good smells for him to investigate, and sometimes old ladies, who didn't know any better, would give him sticky buns to eat.

As he walked past the butcher's shop, the greedy dog started to lick his lips. There in the window was a great big steak. It looked juicy and very good to eat. The greedy dog decided that the steak would make a very nice meal. So he watched and waited outside the shop. Soon one of his favourite old ladies walked down the street and into the butcher's shop. The greedy dog sidled in alongside the unsuspecting old lady. She wanted sausages and mince and goodness knows what else, so while the butcher was looking after her, the greedy dog pounced. He grabbed the steak and galloped out of the shop.

Then there was a great hue and cry. The butcher ran out of his shop, the little old lady fainted, and everyone in the street joined in the chase. But the greedy dog knew all the back streets, and he was soon far away and longing to eat his steak. He ran through the back streets until he came to the canal. He was just about to cross the bridge when he caught sight of another dog, right in front of him, and this dog also had a great juicy steak in his mouth! Well now, you and I know that what he was looking at was his own reflection, but the greedy dog did not know that. All he saw was a second steak that he might have so, with a great fierce bark, he leapt at the other dog.

But instead of gaining another meal, the greedy dog found himself very wet indeed, and he had lost his own steak! It would be good if I could tell you that from that day onwards the greedy dog was better behaved. But I am afraid his manners did not improve, and he is still looking for the other dog…

A Tall Story

An Indian folk tale

Five blind men were once sitting under a shady palm tree by the bank of the River Ganges in India, when they sensed that someone or something had silently crept up and joined them. "Who's there?" asked the first blind man. There was no reply, so he got to his feet and walked forwards with his arms outstretched. After a few steps, his hands hit something flat, rough and solid in front of him. "It's a wall!" he cried.

"Don't be stupid!" cried the second blind man, standing up. "How could someone have built a wall right under our noses without us hearing?" He, too, felt about in front of him. "Aha!" he said, delightedly, as he ran his hands down a hard, smooth, stick-like thing. "It's a spear, definitely a spear!"

At that, the third blind man got up to join them. "A wall and a spear!" he sneered. "Obviously, neither of you have any idea what this thing is." His fingers closed around something tatty and wiggly. "It's nothing more than a piece of old rope!" he laughed.

"How can you say that?" argued the fourth blind man, who had jumped up and joined in without anyone noticing.

"I'm standing here with my arms wrapped around something so big that my fingers are barely touching together. It's a tree trunk, I'm telling you. A tree trunk!"

"I suppose I'll have to settle this," sniffed the fifth blind man, as he rose. He stuck out his hand confidently and grabbed hold of something long and swaying. "HELP!" he shouted. "It's a snake! It's a snake!"

Suddenly, whoops of laughter filled the air and the five blind men heard a little boy giggle, "You're ALL wrong! You're actually holding parts of an elephant – and you all look REALLY SILLY!"

At that, the five blind men all stopped what they were doing. And from that moment on, they never argued again.

Nasreddin Hodja and the Pot

Anon

Nasreddin Hodja went to his neighbour to borrow a large cooking pot for a few days. When he returned it, the neighbour was surprised to find a smaller pot inside, that he had never seen before.

"What's this, Nasreddin?" he said

"Oh, your pot gave birth while in my house," Nasreddin replied, "and naturally as the larger pot is yours, the smaller pot belongs to you also so I have brought it to you."

'What a fool!' thought the man, but he smiled and accepted the pot, pleased at his good fortune.

Some days later, Nasreddin asked if might borrow the pot again. After a few weeks, the neighbour went to Nasreddin's house to ask for it back.

"Oh, I am sorry to tell you," said Nasreddin, "but your pot has died."

"Don't be so foolish" said the neighbour angrily. "Cooking pots don't die!"

"Are you sure?" said Nasreddin. "You didn't seem surprised when you heard it had given birth."

Nasreddin Hodja and the Smell of Soup

Anon

Abeggar was walking along the road of the market. He had begged a small piece of bread for himself, dry and old, and that was all he had to eat that day. Hoping to get something to put on it, he went to a nearby restaurant and begged for a small portion of food, but was ordered out of the inn empty-handed. As he walked out, he stopped to stare at the rich people enjoying the bowls of good savoury soup. He lent over one of the cauldrons and took a deep breath to savour its good smell. At that moment the innkeeper came out and seized his arm.

"Not so fast! You haven't paid!"

"Payment? But I have had nothing," stammered the confused beggar, "I was only enjoying the smell."

"Then you must pay for the smell," insisted the innkeeper. "Do you think I cook my soup for a beggar to steal a smell from? I saw you take it."

The poor beggar had no money to pay, of course, so the innkeeper dragged him off to the Nasreddin Hodja, the judge. Hodja listened most carefully, considering both the innkeeper's angry exclamations, and the beggar's protests that he had taken nothing.

"And you say you have no money?" he asked the poor man.

"Not a penny," stammered the terrified beggar.

Then Hodja turned to the innkeeper.

"So you insist on being paid for the smell?"

"Indeed I do," said the innkeeper.

"Then I myself will pay you," said Hodja.

He drew some coins out of his pocket, and beckoned the innkeeper closer. Hodja held the coins in his hands up to the innkeeper's ear and shook his hand gently so the coins rang together.

"You may go," he said.

The innkeeper said angrily, "but my payment..."

"This man took the smell of the soup," said Hodja, "and you have been paid with the sound of the money. Now go on your way."

Lazy Jack

By Flora Annie Steel

Once upon a time there was a boy whose name was Jack, and he lived with his mother on a common. They were very poor, and the old woman made her living by spinning, but Jack was so useless that he was called Lazy Jack. His mother at last told him that if he did not begin to work for his porridge, she would turn him out.

This roused Jack, and he went out and hired himself for the next day to a neighbouring farmer for a penny, but as he was coming home, never having had any money before, he lost it.

"You stupid boy," said his mother, "you should have put it in your pocket."

"I'll do so another time," replied Jack.

Well, the next day, Jack went out again and hired himself to a cowkeeper, who gave him a jar of milk for his day's work. Jack put the jar into his jacket pocket, spilling it all before he got home.

"Dear me!" said the old woman, "you should have carried it on your head."

"I'll do so another time," said Jack.

So the following day, Jack hired himself again to a farmer, who agreed to give him a cream cheese for his services. In the evening Jack took the cheese, and went home with it on his head. By the time he got home the cheese was all spoilt, part of it being lost, and part matted with his hair.

"You stupid lout," said his mother, "you should have carried it very carefully in your hands."

"I'll do so another time," replied Jack.

Now the next day, Lazy Jack again went out, and hired himself to a baker, who would give him nothing for his work but a large tom-cat. Jack took the cat, and began carrying it very carefully in his hands, but in a short time pussy scratched him so much that he was compelled to let it go.

When he got home, his mother said to him, "You silly fellow, you should have tied it with a string, and dragged it along after you."

"I'll do so another time," said Jack.

So on the following day, Jack hired himself to a butcher, who rewarded him by the handsome present of a shoulder of mutton. Jack took the mutton, tied it with a string, and trailed it along after him in the dirt, so that by the time he got home the meat was completely spoilt. His mother was this time quite out of patience with him.

"You ninney-hammer," said she to her son, "you should have carried it on your shoulder."

"I'll do so another time," replied Jack.

Well, on the Monday, Lazy Jack went once more and hired himself to a cattle-keeper, who gave him a donkey for his trouble. Now though Jack was strong he found it hard to hoist the donkey on his shoulders, but at last he did it, and began walking home.

Now it so happened that he passed a house where a rich man lived with his only daughter, who had never spoken in her life. The doctors said she would never speak till somebody made her laugh. So the father had said that any man who made her laugh would receive her hand in marriage. Now this young lady happened to be looking out of the window when Jack was passing by with the donkey on his shoulders. Well, the sight was so comical that she burst into a fit of laughter, and immediately recovered her speech and hearing. Her father was overjoyed, and fulfilled his promise by marrying her to Lazy Jack, who was thus made a rich gentleman. They lived in a large house, and Jack's mother lived with them in great happiness until she died.

Tikki Tikki Tembo

Anon

Once upon a time in faraway China there lived two brothers, one named Sam, and one named Tikki Tikki Tembo No Sarimbo Hari Kari Bushkie Perry Pem Do Hai Kai Pom Pom Nikki No Meeno Dom Barako.

Now one day the two brothers were playing near the well in their garden when Sam fell into the well, and Tikki Tikki Tembo No Sarimbo Hari Kari Bushkie Perry Pem Do Hai Kai Pom Pom

28

Nikki No Meeno Dom Barako ran to his mother, shouting, "Quick, Sam has fallen into the well."

"What?" cried the mother, "Sam has fallen into the well? Run and tell father!"

Together they ran to the father and cried, "Quick, Sam has fallen into the well."

"Sam has fallen into the well?" cried the father. "Run and tell the gardener!"

Then they all ran to the gardener and shouted, "Quick, Sam has fallen into the well."

"Sam has fallen into the well?" cried the gardener, and then he quickly fetched a ladder and pulled the poor boy from the well, who was wet, cold and frightened.

Some time afterward the two brothers were again playing near the well. This time Tikki Tikki Tembo No Sarimbo Hari Kari Bushkie Perry Pem Do Hai Kai Pom Pom Nikki No Meeno Dom Barako fell into the well, and Sam ran to his mother, shouting, "Quick, Tikki Tikki Tembo No Sarimbo Hari Kari Bushkie Perry Pem Do Hai Kai Pom Pom Nikki No Meeno Dom Barako has fallen into the well."

"What?" cried the mother, "Tikki Tikki Tembo No Sarimbo Hari Kari Bushkie Perry Pem Do Hai Kai Pom Pom Nikki No Meeno Dom Barako has fallen into the well? Run and tell father!"

Together they ran to the father and cried, "Quick, Tikki Tikki Tembo No Sarimbo Hari Kari Bushkie Perry Pem Do Hai Kai Pom Pom Nikki No Meeno Dom Barako has fallen into the well."

"Tikki Tikki Tembo No Sarimbo Hari Kari

Bushkie Perry Pem Do Hai Kai Pom Pom Nikki No Meeno Dom Barako has fallen into the well?" cried the father. "Run and tell the gardener!"

So they all ran to the gardener and shouted, "Quick, Tikki Tikki Tembo No Sarimbo Hari Kari Bushkie Perry Pem Do Hai Kai Pom Pom Nikki No Meeno Dom Barako has fallen into the well."

"Tikki Tikki Tembo No Sarimbo Hari Kari Bushkie Perry Pem Do Hai Kai Pom Pom Nikki No Meeno Dom Barako has fallen into the well?" cried the gardener, and then he quickly fetched a ladder and pulled Tikki Tikki Tembo No Sarimbo Hari Kari Bushkie Perry Pem Do Hai Kai Pom Pom Nikki No Meeno Dom Barako from the well, but the poor boy had been in the water so long that he had drowned.

And from that time forth, the Chinese have given their children short names.

The Husband who was to Mind the House

By Peter Christen Asbjørnsen

Once upon a time there was a man who was so bad tempered and cross that he never thought his wife did anything right in the house. One evening, in hay-making time, he came home, scolding and shouting.

"Dear love, don't be so angry, that's a good man," said his wife, "tomorrow let's change jobs. I'll go out with the mowers and mow, and you can mind the house at home."

The Husband who was to Mind the House

Yes, the husband thought that would do very well. He was quite willing, he said.

So early the next morning, his wife took a scythe over her neck, and went out into the hay field with the mowers and began to mow, but the man was to mind the house, and do the work at home.

First of all he wanted to churn the butter, but when he had churned awhile, he got thirsty, and went down to the cellar to tap a barrel of ale. He had just knocked in the bung, and was putting in the tap, when he heard the pig come into the kitchen above. As as fast as he could, he ran up the cellar steps, with the tap in his hand, to keep the pig from upsetting the churn, but when he got there, the pig had already knocked the churn over, and was rolling in the cream on the floor.

He got so angry that he quite forgot the ale barrel, and ran at the pig as hard as he could. He caught it and gave it such a powerful kick that he killed it on the spot. Then he remembered he had the tap in his hand, but when he got down to the cellar, all the ale had run out of the barrel.

Then he went into the milk shed and found enough cream left to fill the churn again, and so he began to churn, for they had to have butter at dinner. When he had churned a bit, he remembered that their milk cow was still shut up in the barn, and hadn't had a bit to eat or a drop to drink all morning, although the sun was high. It occurred to him that it was too far to take her down to the meadow, so he'd just get her up on the roof, for it was a sod roof, and a fine crop of grass was growing there.

But he couldn't leave the churn, for his baby was crawling about on the floor. 'If I leave it,' he thought, 'the child will tip it over.' So he took the churn on his back and went out, but then he thought he'd better draw water for the cow before he put her on the roof. So he picked up a bucket to draw water out of the well, but, as he stooped over the edge of the well, all the cream ran out of the churn over his shoulder and down into the well.

Now it was near dinner time, and he hadn't even got the butter yet, so he thought he'd best boil the porridge, and filled the pot with water and hung it over the fire. When he had done that, it occurred to him that the cow might fall off the roof. So he tied one end of a rope to the cow's neck. He slipped the other end down the chimney and tied it around his own leg. Then he had to hurry, for the water was now boiling in the pot, and he had still to grind the oatmeal. As he began to grind away, the cow fell off the roof, dragging the man up the chimney. There he stuck fast, and the cow hung halfway down the wall.

Now the wife waited for her husband to call her home to dinner, but he never came. At last she thought she'd waited long enough, and went home. But when she got home and saw the cow hanging there, she ran up and cut the rope with her scythe. When she did this, her husband fell down from within the chimney. When the old woman came inside, she found him upside down with his head in the porridge pot.

Teeny-tiny

An English folk tale

Once upon a time there lived a teeny-tiny old woman. She lived in a teeny-tiny house in a teeny-tiny street with a teeny-tiny cat. One day the teeny-tiny woman decided to go out for a teeny-tiny walk. She put on her teeny-tiny boots and her teeny-tiny bonnet, and off she set.

When she had walked a teeny-tiny way down the teeny-tiny street, she went through a teeny-tiny gate into a teeny-tiny graveyard, which was a teeny-tiny shortcut to the teeny-tiny meadow. Well, she had only taken a few teeny-tiny steps when she saw a teeny-tiny bone lying on top of a teeny-tiny grave. She thought that would do very well to make some teeny-tiny soup for supper so she put the teeny-tiny bone in her teeny-tiny pocket and went home at once to her teeny-tiny house.

Now the teeny-tiny woman was tired when she reached her teeny-tiny house so she did not make the teeny-tiny soup immediately, but put the teeny-tiny bone into her teeny-tiny cupboard. Then she sat in her teeny-tiny chair and put her teeny-tiny feet up and had a teeny-tiny sleep. But she had only been asleep a teeny-tiny time when she woke up at the sound of a teeny-tiny voice coming from her teeny-tiny cupboard. The teeny-tiny voice said, "Where is my teeny-tiny bone?"

Well, the teeny-tiny woman was a teeny-tiny bit frightened so she wrapped her teeny-tiny shawl round her teeny-tiny head and went to sleep again. She had only been asleep a teeny-tiny time

when the teeny-tiny voice came from the teeny-tiny cupboard again, a teeny-tiny bit louder this time. "Where is my teeny-tiny bone?"

The teeny-tiny woman was a teeny-tiny bit more frightened than last time so she hid under the teeny-tiny cushions, but she could not go back to sleep, not even a teeny-tiny bit. Then the teeny-tiny voice came again and this time it was even a teeny-tiny bit louder. "Where is my teeny-tiny bone?"

This time the teeny-tiny woman sat up in her teeny-tiny chair and said in her loudest teeny-tiny voice, "TAKE IT!"

There was a teeny-tiny silence, and then a teeny-tiny ghost ran out of the teeny-tiny house, down the teeny-tiny street, through the teeny-tiny gate into the teeny-tiny graveyard – with the teeny-tiny bone clutched very tightly in its teeny-tiny hand! And the teeny-tiny woman never took even a teeny-tiny walk there ever again!